The Bear Who Couldn't Sleep

For my mother, with love. C.N.

To my mother: for her
endless love and support. V.N.

The Bear Who Couldn't Sleep

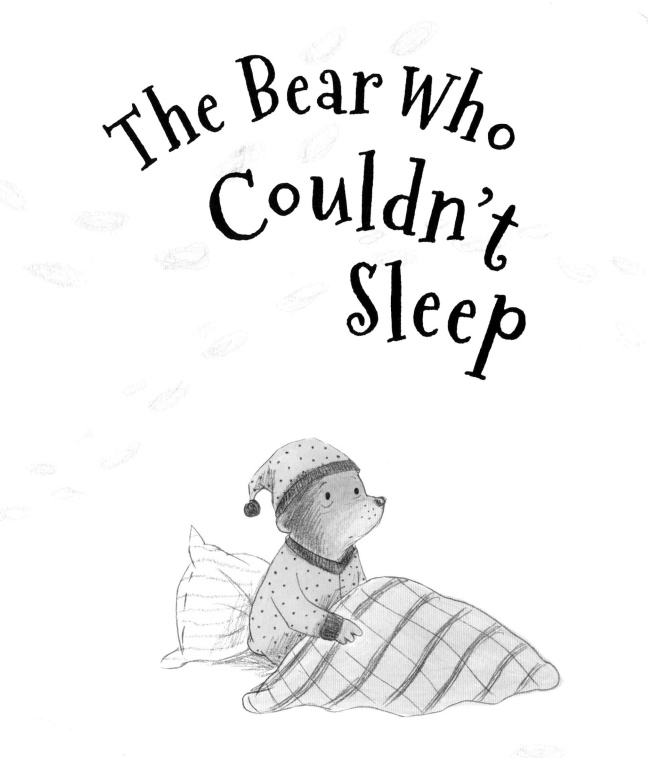

by Caroline Nastro

illustrated by Vanya Nastanlieva

North South

There once was a bear who could not sleep in the winter. While his mother and brothers slept, Bear stayed awake. The leaves fell, the snow came, but still Bear could not sleep.

He left his home to visit his neighbors,
but everyone was sleeping.

So Bear kept walking,

until he arrived at a very big city . . .

. . . where no one was sleeping, even in the middle of winter! There was so much to see and so much to do!

Bear went up and down,

and back and forth,

and to and fro, and all around.

He was so busy, so busy,
so busy, so busy!

He saw the famous Statue of Liberty.

The opera was just wonderful, the food outstanding!

Bear loved the city that never sleeps!

He visited the Metropolitan Museum of Art,
and fell in love with a Jackson Pollock.
He could stay here all winter!

No need to rest!

He could keep going,

and going,

and going . . .

if only he weren't getting . . .

SO . . . SO . . .
SLEEPY!

He found a nice bench on Broadway,

that wasn't exactly the perfect spot.

He looked for a place to rest in Times Square, but the cars and the taxis kept honking and honking.

He found a quiet spot by
the *Barosaurus* in the
Museum of Natural History,

but a guard woke him up and said, "I am sorry, sir. The museum is closing."

He curled up next to a tree
in Central Park, but a park
ranger told him, "You cannot
stay here after dark."

So Bear left the city that never sleeps, and he walked

and he walked, and he walked, and he walked . . .

. . . back to the forest and his home, where he snuggled
in next to his mother and brothers. There were no
taxis to wake him, no park rangers to shoo him.

It was just Bear and his dreams and the quiet sounds of the winter.

Text copyright © 2016 by Caroline Nastro
Illustrations copyright © 2016 by Vanya Nastanlieva
First published in the United States, Great Britain, Canada, Australia,
and New Zealand in 2016 by NorthSouth Books, Inc., an imprint of
NordSüd Verlag AG, CH-8005 Zürich, Switzerland.

Distributed in the United States by NorthSouth Books, Inc., New York 10016.
Library of Congress Cataloging-in-Publication Data is available.
ISBN: 978-0-7358-4268-7
Printed in Latvia by Livonia Print, Riga, April 2016.
1 3 5 7 9 • 10 8 6 4 2
www.northsouth.com

MIX
Paper from
responsible sources
FSC® C002795
FSC
www.fsc.org